IMMORTALITY FOR YOU

A LIFE-SAVING BOOK 200 YEARS AHEAD OF ITS TIME.

DOCTOR RICHARD PARSONS

IMMORTALITY FOR YOU

A LIFE-SAVING BOOK 200 YEARS AHEAD OF ITS TIME.

MEMOIRS
Cirencester

Published by Memoirs

MEMOIRS
PUBLISHING

25 Market Place, Cirencester, Gloucestershire, GL7 2NX
info@memoirsbooks.co.uk www.memoirspublishing.com

ISBN: 978-1909304215

TABLE OF CONTENTS

CHAPTER ONE

RESURRECTING THE DEAD

THERE IS RESURRECTION by technology, called cryogenics. The way scientists can attempt to rescue a dead man is to freeze the body, then hope that through the progress of the world technology will be sufficiently advanced to thaw the individual and cure him of whatever ailment caused his death. This will be a method of 'curing' death in the future.

An American company has actually undertaken to store frozen bodies for 200 years. Recently the company has been freezing heads, as a cheaper alternative. Of course, the chance of scientists curing the frozen bodies of death is one in a million. However, the wizard - more about the wizard later - has made a breakthrough by storing the dead bodies on film - by freezing the dead bodies, then removing a 1000th of a millimetre, then taking a picture of the remaining body; then removing another part of the body and taking a picture of the remaining part. The process continues until a total of two million images are taken and stored on film, before being stored in a machine. This in effect means the entire body and head images are stored on film.

The image of a man or woman is an organ, or an organic blueprint, telling the public what type of individual he or she is - whether simple or intelligent, mean, happy or sad. The internal image of the body tells scientists how the body functions. A complete 100 per cent image is that of a fully composed organ. The image organ is composed, while the rest of the body is decomposed. This means the body is undecomposed. The body can remain undecomposed forever.

Imagine your body is fully composed after you are dead. You will not have any feelings until you are aware your body remains composed forever and ever. Then you will experience a contented feeling. Now imagine your body is fully composed temporarily. Until your body becomes undecomposed forever and ever, you may experience a slight pleasurable feeling - by being aware your body is undecomposed for ever and ever. If the body is fully composed forever a slight feeling of happiness will prevail. If the body is undecomposed forever, there will be a lesser lovely feeling. At the age of 60 men and women know they are not going to be resurrected. They know they are going to decompose. There is no proof they are not going to be resurrected, and there is no proof they are going to decompose; but they continue to believe, and nurture hope, until they have proof. At the age of 65 they have sufficient proof they are going to decompose - merely by looking at themselves in the mirror! They may conclude they have proof they are not going to be resurrected. The solution is a body remaining undecomposed for ever.

The feeling of love is lost at the age of 55. When the body is undecomposed the body is never fully in the earth. The word *die* means departed in earth. When the body is undecomposed the body doesn't fully die. This gives rise to a lovely feeling that never ends at all - not for ages, whether it be at the age of 80, 90, 120, 140, or earlier - at 55 or 60 - all ages, in fact. A 75-year-old man is resurrected morally and intellectually by knowing he is never going to fully die, then decompose. From the age of 55 onwards men and women never become aged. They never become morally and intellectually dead. From the age of 55 to the time they depart they never lose awareness of resurrection.

The images of men and women are stored in a machine. Then 400 or 40,000 years later, scientists study the images and replace the bodily parts - the parts of flesh - on film with artificial parts in an artificial body. After the first million men and women have been resurrected in this way, scientists program a machine to recognise the different brain and body parts. The machine is programmed to determine what the individual member parts can do - the substance the parts are made of; how dense the parts are; what chemical composition the parts have; what size the parts are - and so on. The machine then replaces the parts of flesh on film, substituting them with artificial parts in an artificial body.

The resurrection of the dead ideally takes place in space colonies, in space. This is really the only way the dead population can be resurrected - simply because there is not enough room on earth. Rockets are not the most appropriate form of transportation for space-colony construction. Fortunately the wizard (more about him later) has invented an advanced space vehicle, capable of lifting off and flying to an earth orbit - cheaper and one million-fold more reliable than a rocket vehicle. The governments are not able to make available resurrection technology to the public until the governments have the technology. Another and superior technology will be required by scientists - an advanced computer with eyes. This book issues details of how such a computer works. The general direction and basic details of how to rescue and revive a dead body are straightforward and methodical. Minor innovation is all that is required. The individual body parts are made. Remember that years ago the technology of today might have been considered an impossible fantasy. The progress the world has made has caused the public to realise almost anything is possible in the future.

At the time of resurrection the thoughts and past actions are seen by the police and scientists. The police will know exactly what crime was committed by those resurrected. This will be achieved by scanning the brain images of one billion men and women in advance to provide a bank of information against which to measure the criminal potential of those resurrected. All of the one billion men and women scanned to provide the bank of images would be made to make the same speech and body actions. Scientists and the police will therefore recognise the speech and body actions of those resurrected because those particular speech and body actions will match the same speech and body actions as the preliminary persons that were scanned. This inevitably will assist the authorities to identify and understand the body actions and speech the criminal is likely to make. As a result killers will be aware they will almost certainly be caught when they are resurrected. One in a million killers is likely to kill. One in a million thieves will almost certainly engage in theft. Thus if the government accepts resurrection as inevitable, the government will be in a position to prevent crime. Advocating resurrection will encourage less crime. The government is well advised to act for the future by taking this book seriously once it is issued. The government will know, and the criminal will know, that there can be no escape for committing serious crime in this life, for justice will be meted out in the future. If persons commit very sick crimes, they will be aware they shall be caught - for capture and conviction will be inevitable when they are resurrected. Death is no escape, and is not final. In other words, their brains will be scanned, and the police will discover what they have done. From that point they shall be left dead forever.

The issue of this book has provided an opportunity for resurrection. If the government doesn't act on it, it would be making a serious mistake. The general direction and basic details of how dead bodies can be resurrected have been withheld by the wizard of this book. I use the word *wizard* because I don't know of any other appropriate title or word to call myself. When the government pays the demands of the wizard, full details of resurrection will be issued - for to resurrect the dead, scientists require the technological know-how. Part of the technology required is an advanced sight-seeing computer that recognises one hundred million body parts a second. Five years ago scientists developed a computer that makes one hundred trillion or one billion calculations a second. The computers of the future will be programmed to recognise different brain and body parts, then program a machine to manufacture the parts. In essence the instructions as to how the computer works will be found in this book.

Another thing scientists will require is an inexpensive earth-to-earth orbit space vehicle; also a walking, talking robot that does any industrial job as well as any intellectual job. Scientists will be able to construct the first robot within ten years - perhaps within eight years. Trillions of robots in space will resurrect the dead. If the public are morally dead, the public will in effect arrive into the afterlife dead. If the public are dead in this life, the public will almost certainly be dead in the afterlife. If a man proves he is undead in the afterlife, he will be undead in this life. If men and women do exactly the same thing again, they are dead. If they don't relive the same actions, have the same moral feelings or thoughts again, they are morally alive. When they are morally alive they are undead. When they are forced to do what is disgusting and they are aware they are doing what is disgusting intellectually, they are not doing what is disgusting morally. They are never forced morally. When they are forced to live the same life again, they are not living the same lifespan again morally. This means when they live repeated lifespans, they are not absolutely living repeated lifespans. Then they are undead. When they live the same lifespans again and are punished, morally, they deserve what they are experiencing. Then there is no resistance, for they are morally dead. If they know they are living the same lifespan again, they are not extinguished. When they are not extinguished, they have an afterlife. When they have an afterlife, there are signs of the afterlife in this life.

An undecomposed body is the sign the individual has an afterlife. A fully decomposed body has no signs of an afterlife. When persons are not extinguished they have an undecomposed body, forever. This means they have a satisfying, positive feeling of awareness, for ever, an experience of everlasting love. Living the same life again means the afterlife is, in effect, this life. That is why they have love forever. There is no incentive to do bad things since the undecomposed body has no effect - the resurrected persons don't earn love by doing bad or by hurting others and committing crimes. If they engaged in bad acts, they would fear living the same life again. Then, in effect, they will be in hell. When they do good acts they don't fear living the same lifespan again, so in effect they go to heaven. It's a choice between hell on earth, and heaven on earth. The more they hurt others and commit crime, the more they fear living the same lifespan again. The less they commit crime and hurt others, the less they fear living the same lifespan. Proof of living repeated lifespans informs an undecomposed body for ever.

Scientists and doctors resurrect the dead by recreating the brain and internal organs and muscles inside a machine twenty feet long and ten feet wide. The internal parts can be increased in size by a scale of twenty. This makes manufacture of the parts easier. The moving, walking, talking body receives messages and signals from the machine. The signals and messages tell the body when to move, walk and talk. Thoughts from the brain are transmitted to the body one hundred miles away. What the artificial body hears and sees is transmitted to the machine. The artificial body has exactly the same thoughts as a man or woman of flesh. The artificial body has the same feelings; it eats, drinks, sleeps, walks, rests, has active sex, fun; in short, it has all the same functions as a body of flesh, the only difference being that the body is artificial. An advanced computer that can recognise a billion brain parts a second accelerates the resurrection operation.

CHAPTER TWO

PROOF OF REPEATED LIFESPANS

A **MAN IS CONSIDERED** departed when his body is dead. The 'nothing' he becomes is the same as the 'nothing' he was a million years ago - or forever ago. The 'nothing' he is has the same mechanism or motion, and circumstances as the 'nothing' he was forever ago. One in a million trillion star systems with planets are exactly the same as the earth and sun were billions of years ago - perhaps forever ago. Thus the man is born again because the 'nothing' on the identical earth, sun and planets is exactly the same 'nothing', having exactly the same mechanism, circumstance, chance and motion as he had before; and so the same man is born again on the identical earth.

The number of stars and planets in the universe continue forever as an unlimited number of stars. This tells us that, according to the law of averages, there is a planet exactly the same as the earth, having exactly the same solar system. When men and women are living the same lifespan in terms of love and happiness, they are not living the same lifespan again. When they know they are living the same lifespan again and they are moving forward in terms of love and happiness, they are not living the lifespan again, or repeating the same lifespan. When they are moving forward in terms of pain and suffering, they are lost. When they are lost, they are living the same lifespan again, living the same lifespan again by fear, suffering, pain. Then the loss is absolute. *Loss*!

When they tell the truth they have the ability to come terms with living repeated lifespans. If they use this ability, they will realise the public can or had lifespans that are worse. Crime makers will know if they commit a crime. They run the risk of spending a large part of their lives in prison forever. When the public are aware of the truth, they will feel better off. By expecting absolute death, suffering, grief, the truth will shock them, for they shall come to the realisation and know there is no immediate heaven - perhaps any heaven. Then they will realise the suffering and pain isn't absolute, for they did not die.

Proof of living repeated lives or lifespans means the public will have the incentive to check their direction, knowing if they make mistakes they are pre-empting death, grief and suffering in the future. Do good, go to heaven; do bad, go to hell. Go to heaven, don't fear death forever. Go to hell, fear death forever. Smoking is bad. Bullying others is bad. The public will make fewer and fewer mistakes, knowing they are pre-empting less grief in the future for themselves.

Proof of living repeated lifespans is very effective crime prevention. All forms of suicide will be prevented. Murder and theft, too, as well as other crimes will be reduced. The bodies of men and women will either depart or live on forever. Living repeated lifespans comes about when the public are not aware of where they are going. If a man knows he is living the same lifespan forever, he is not lost. He is not lost - because he is aware in the future his house and home will still be here. The road and street will still be here. So will the people, plants, trees, buildings. He knows he will be walking on the same streets, sitting in the same home, living in the same world. Then he has a sense of growth for the future and a sense of direction for the past. He knows in the past he will be living the same lifespan again, doing the same things and seeing the same things, again. He is aware in the future he will be walking along the same street, living in the same house, talking to the same people. He is aware he will be doing all this forever; meaning, he is not lost in the future and is not lost in the past. From the time he knows he is living the same lifespan again, he is not lost, going back to an undecomposed body.

When the bodies of members of the public don't decompose, they have the feeling of love forever. At the age of 55 there is proof of no love. They have proof they are going to die. The ageing process then is undeniable. By proof of repeated lifespans and no death, love continues forever. When the body is dead but still composed, it is on the earth forever. The person therefore doesn't die. When the dead body is undecomposed forever on earth, they don't die - because the body is not fully decomposed. This is why there is what we might call 'magical credit' by an undecomposed body. The composed or preserved part of the body is what engenders a feeling of no loss. At the age of 55 people have a dead look on their faces. A morally dead man will have a 'dead' appearance. If love is lost, the appearance is dead. If love is not lost he is morally alive. Then he appears morally alive. Because he is morally alive he has proof he is not going to die. This is why he has a feeling of love at the age of 55. A 70-year-old man will have the face of a 70-year-old man, not the face and body of a 54-year-old man. Having love at the age of 70 transforms the body and face to that of a 54-year-old man or woman. If they have the appearance of a 70-year-old, there is no sign of love in their faces, or in the sight of their bodies.

At the age of 70 there is no sign of love. If there is no sign of love, there is no love. They know love is a fantasy. At the age of 55 there is already no genuine fantasy left. 'Fantasy by disorder', one could say, a 55-year-old person accepts - fantasy that might still generate a sense of genuine happiness and love. Nevertheless a mature 55-year-old rejects such fantasy. The absence of love is proof they are going to decompose, then die. When they have proof they are not going to die, they keep the body and face of a younger man. What they think and feel at the age of 70 is not love.

You may ask how they stay young - by the proof they shall never die. This book explains how the public stop ageing at the age of 55.

CHAPTER THREE

THE ADVANCED SIGHT-SEEING COMPUTER

THE **RECOGNITION** of the tiny body parts stored on film for resurrection is done by a special computer. This is how the computer works. The computer takes external pictures of objects. Then the picture on film is developed. A row of pressure sensitive styluses, the same as stylus needles of old-fashioned record players or hi-fi sets, travel up and down over the protruding emulsion of the image of the film - just as a stylus needle travels up and down along the groove of a 12-inch record. The styluses measure different protruding shapes and bumps of the protruding emulsion on the film, giving the computer any recognised understanding of the objects and images it sees. The computer is placed inside a dark room. Then it is shown individual brain and body parts. After the intelligence is told what the particular brain or body is, the computer records the brain and body parts. Then, when the computer sees a similar brain or body part, the memory of the computer tells the computer what the part is. The computer determines what the part is, by being told there are parameters or limits of what shape and size the brain and body parts can have. Then the computer is programmed to know whether the part fits the approximate shape and size. When the computer is in the dark room it is made to 'see' one single sight of an image at a time. This way the computer doesn't get confused by 'seeing' many objects at the same time, causing the computer to assume all the images and objects on film are part of one image on film. The computer is made to recognise the image within one ten-thousandth of a second.

CHAPTER FOUR

THE LOOK OF YOUTH

GOING BACK to the undecomposed body: by an undecomposed body the feeling of love continues. This means the love the person feels is visibly detected. The expression of love and happiness continues at all ages - in the expression on their faces, the position or attitude of their bodies (their body language), the clothes they wear. This is the situation when there is no sight, or awareness, of absolute old age. This stems from knowing they are going to have undecomposed bodies - and they don't die. At the age of 70 part of such a person appears young; there is something about him or her, preventing the appearance of absolute old age. Love is still there, and this means parts of these individuals are standing still and not ageing. The rest of them are ageing. Parts of them remains still, or static, so in a sense parts of them remain young, or at any rate younger; this means they are ageing at a slower rate because parts of them are resisting the ageing process, producing what one might call a dragging effect. This means they are slowing down ageing, ageing at a slower rate. If they live long enough they will stop ageing, then feel the full effect of one hundred per cent happiness. This means they have a destination. That's the destination before they depart, which determines the destination after they depart. Before they depart they see the way out of the grave. The way out is a feeling not felt in the same way twice.

CHAPTER FIVE

THE UNEXTINCT HUMAN RACE

UNHUMAN MOTION continues forever. Men send a spacecraft towards another star, eventually arriving at another star thousands of millions of years from now. The spacecraft has artificial motion, and artificial motion continues forever. The gravity of the spacecraft has the effect, however minutely at first, of pulling planets and debris to a different position; then those stars and planets pull stars and planets; then more stars and planets are pulled to a different position; then all the stars and planets and dust and debris in the galaxy are moved to a different position. Then this galaxy moves another galaxy. Then these galaxies are moved - until the motion effect continues forever.

There is no limit as to how weak the gravitational pull can be to initiate this on-going effect. The pull of gravity can be reduced forever. The motion effect forms a new presence in the universe. The motion of the spacecraft functions the same as a machine functioning forever. The spacecraft forms perpetual motion. The effect from the spacecraft is detectable and the spacecraft is part of the effect. This is why part of the spacecraft is detected forever - because of this the spacecraft doesn't cease to exist.

Technology is an extension of the human body. The car 'runs' faster and the boat 'swims' faster. The aircraft 'jumps' higher. Men are part of the extension and women are part of men. The extension doesn't die. This means a part of men and women don't die. The effect of the spacecraft motion is on the grave forever. Men and women have the same body and genes as famous scientists and inventors. The public are part of the achievement. Part of the record of the public is on the grave by the motion effect of the spacecraft. The record is the extension of the memory. The memory is the soul. The extension of the soul continues forever. Limited motion is not able to form unlimited motion. The motion of animals is not able to escape the earth's sun and solar system. The motion of animals is claimed by the earth and the sun. The motion of men and women don't fully move with the earth and sun. This is because the spacecraft escapes the solar system, causing motion effect amongst the stars and planets forever.

As a result men and women are unmoved. Animals are under the control of the earth and the sun while the motion of animals never was. British men and women sing a song - the lyrics tell us that 'we shall not be moved'. We shall not be moved. Just like a team that's going to win the FA cup, we shall not be moved! It takes forever to make forever - the motion of men and women come from forever ago, an unlimited number of years ago.

The motion of animals begins and the motion of animals ends. Animals are not able to generate perpetual motion. The spacecraft forms perpetual motion from the motion formed by men. Part of the genes of men and women lives on forever; as a result men and women never become fully extinct by detection of the motion of the spacecraft. Part of the technology is motion. Part of the genes of men and women is motion. If there is no motion, the substance is not able to grow; so no motion, no gene, and the genes of men and women become extinct. Then men and women are extinct.

The unextinct have supernatural connections. The sight of the spacecraft motion effect is the first of a supernatural manifestation; detection and seeing forever through happiness and love become part of what you see, then become part of another world, become part of forever and immortality. There is a sense of infinity and by becoming part of forever we don't die. The sight of forever through happiness and love is a cool, refreshing sight of darkness in light. What is part of forever never ends. It never dies.

Different chemical reactions take place inside the brain, causing unhuman thoughts. The thoughts overflow to the mind forming unhuman speech. The speech overflows to the voice, forming unhuman body actions. The body actions overflow forming unhuman internal or visceral body actions. Then the body forms an unhuman world.

The achievement of the wizard is not human. This is not a world without end. First the public see a beginning, then the public see an end. There was no proof of forever. When they don't detect forever, they don't have forever. If an animal saw the world by happiness, the animal becomes part of what the animal sees. What the spectator sees, the spectator is part of. Chemical reactions take place inside the brain. Chemical reactions are physical; consequently the spectator is a physical being, part of what he or she sees. The sight of forever forms an unhuman expression; this is because forever is the opposite of the beginning and the end. Unhuman expression comes from an unhuman body. The physical body forms physical body expressions. Prolonged unhuman sight leads to unhuman expression; unhuman expression is an unhuman body. If expression is physical, then part of the body is not human. When the wizard is expected to look happy, he looks sad. When the wizard is expected to look sad, he looks happy. The higher the species the nearer to unhuman expression they are; the nearer to an unhuman body they are. Mortals have higher intelligence - they anticipate life after death.

CHAPTER SIX

A FLYING SAUCER FOR THE WORLD

IN **ORDER** for the world to last forever, there has got to be unlimited energy and cheap, fast star travel. The unlimited energy has already been discussed in this book. Also, the wizard has issued a flying saucer technology. Scientists and the government are now ready for a quantum leap towards a human betterment for the world. The only way the public can be resurrected is by cheap space travel - thanks to the technology the wizard has invented; by this means one can travel to the stars - by nuclear power and energy.

The wizard is withholding a different type of flying saucer - one that can fly from earth to an earth orbit. This form of travel is 1000 times cheaper than a rocket; and 1000,000 times more reliable and safer. The technology allows the construction of space colonies. This is the only way the public can be resurrected; there is no other way, simply because there would not be enough room on earth to contain all the population living by recorded speech forever. Resurrection of the public is therefore not possible - not until scientists have cheap reliable earth orbital space vehicles, and not unless they get to the stars fast and cheaply; otherwise humans will become extinct - simply because all the water in the solar system will eventually be used up. They are not able to travel to other stars by rocket. The population can live forever thanks to star travel. Unless they have a way of getting to the stars, there will be extinction.

The flying saucer invention in this book is what scientists call a closed system - or a star drive, or hyper drive. The vehicle travels without pushing on or against anything. Cars push on the ground, boats push and pull on water; aircraft push on the air. Scientists say rockets push on their exhaust gases. The flying saucer pushes on itself, just as a woman on roller skates moves across the hall by pulling her own hair; or a man travelling from earth to the moon by pulling his own bootlaces.

The vehicle levitates. Scientists say that levitation is fantasy, not physics. They don't believe levitation is possible.

The wizard calls the flying saucer a space drive, or a magneto drive. How it works is explained in the pages that follow. The other more advanced magneto drive is not disclosed. You, the reader, have got to make certain this book is issued to the appropriate persons - the police, doctors, solicitors, media, newspapers, scientists. You may say that you are leaving this responsibility to other readers, but they may well be leaving the responsibility to you. Together this makes no progress.

THE MAGNETO DRIVE

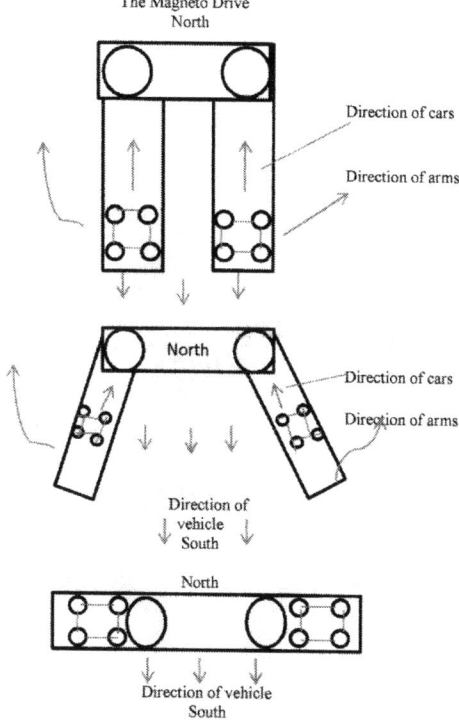

As both arms swing open, the cars arrive at the end of the arms. Both arms are fixed to the vehicle. The vehicle travels south when the cars are travelling north. The arms stop swinging when they reach the horizontal position. The force of the cars travelling along the arms is greater than the swinging-out force of the arms. The cars travel from one side of the arms to the other by brute force.

CHAPTER SEVEN

THE UNDECOMPOSED

THE **UNDECOMPOSED** are authors and writers. Their achievement doesn't allow them to panic. Space scientists, rocket scientists and space advocates constitute a space society, and are members of that society. They have an unextinct gene forming a united soul. Authors and writers have an unextinct gene by virtue of their personal motion. The soul of a space scientist is undecomposed. The spirit is unerazed. The mind is unobliterated. The voice is unmoved. The united heart is unmoved; the single heart is moved. Authors and writers have an undead soul and an unmoved heart. They have an unmoved united desire. The heart is calm, cool.

Authors and writers are, you might say, united in a tiny heart of calm. They have a trace per cent of calm and so remain cool. When the water is boiling, the water is not settled; when the water is cool the water is not moving of its own accord; no panic ensues, because the water is not 100 per cent boiling. When the water boils, the kettle whistles; no absolute boiling means no whistle. No whistle signifies a state of calm. Because they have a heart there is no end. Consequently there is no absolute grief or suffering.

You might also say authors and writers are in hell, paradoxically because they have hope in hell. There's no absolute grief, suffering, excruciation. Those members of the public who create through writing suffer absolute grief or suffering. The undecomposed are aware they are not in absolute grief or suffering. They are not aware they are undecomposed. The undecomposed have rest, and they rest in peace; from the womb to the tomb, they rest.

Parents read books. The books they read gave an effect on them. The effect is detected in their speech and voice. Then the effect is passed on to their children and friends, then those children and friends pass the effect on to their children and friends; then those children and friends pass the effect on until the effect is passed on forever. The effect is reduced forever. There is no limit how small the effect becomes.

CHAPTER EIGHT

THE YOUTH OF RESURRECTION

AN OLD MAN 80 years of age is given the artificial body of an 18-year-old youth. If the parts are the same as the old damaged wrinkled brittle parts, the man has an artificial body just like that of an old man. When the parts of his new body acquire the same function as those of an old man, they are made to function without any damage, without any wrinkles, without any brittle bones, without blocked body tissue. The old man now has the artificial body of an 18-year-old youth.

At the age of 44 persons still nurture the hope of becoming young again. Then at the age of 45 they have proof they are getting old. At the age of 48 they have proof they are never going to get young; but by their awareness of resurrection artificial rejuvenation is foreseeable. The hope of getting young continues through all ages 60 - 70 - 80 - 100 - 129 - all ages. The ageing process is caused by seeing and hearing and detecting pain, with suffering in the future. When persons detect the threat of grief, pain, suffering, they flinch and become tense. When the sponge is tense, squeezed tight, the sponge doesn't absorb water. As people get older and experience more pain, grief, suffering, the more they fear. The more tense they become the less water they absorb. The less water they absorb, the older they become; and the older they become the more they fear pain and suffering and grief.

Babies have more water in their bodies than ten-year-olds, and ten-year-olds have more water in their bodies than thirty-year-olds; thirty-year-olds have more water in their bodies than old men and women. The older they become the more water they lose. The more water they lose the older they look.

The future for a child is grief, not joy; they know they have more time than adults; this is why children are more relaxed. Children walk and run more, expressing spontaneous joy and happiness more easily than those older than themselves. The public grow old because they see and hear, and become aware of pain and suffering for themselves in the future. The public are dying from the first day they are born. According to scientists men and women begin to die at the age of thirty, but this is not correct. A ten-year-old is 'harder' than a baby. You can say then that the ten-year-old has aged by discredit - that the ten-year-old is getting old. He doesn't have proof until he is 45 years of age that he is indeed ageing.

In the distant future men and women and children foresee grief, suffering, pain, death, destruction. If in the distant future they foresee an end of suffering and pain, realising they are going to have happiness and joy forever, they will realise more and more fulfilment in the present time. The immediate future is grief, suffering - but the distant future is happiness, joy. Yesterday the public was living for the now, anticipating what was about to happen in the immediate now but also in the future, telling themselves the delight is going to last - yet knowing the delight is going to end.

Then there is the next high. Each time the delight ends they assume the grief and suffering in the very distant future is going to last forever; they have no proof but they have hope, though the assumption of future death causes the public to become tense. By awareness of resurrection by artificial body, however, they assume genuine happiness in the very distant future in spite of grief and suffering in the immediate future.

Those who assume rejuvenation and resurrection travel in the opposite direction of getting old. As a result they are rejuvenated and resurrected - in the distant future. At the age of 35 they are not getting younger; at the age of 40 they are no longer young; at the age of 45 they are manifestly getting old. By assuming happiness and love in the distant future they morally get younger; when this continues they get intellectually younger - and after a longer period of time they stop ageing, then get physically younger. If their bodies of flesh function for a long enough period of time, they eventually get younger, though exactly when this happens is not known. By knowing and being confident they will live long enough to rejuvenate, they have love and happiness to look forward to - in this life as well as in the afterlife, the life they will have after they are resurrected.

CHAPTER NINE

THE IMPLICATIONS OF STAYING UNDEAD
BY RECORDED SPEECH

WHEN THE GOAL of speech is scored, it makes no difference how the goal is achieved. Speech is not achieved by a dead body. When the goal is happiness, it makes no difference how the goal is scored. Happiness is earned fair and square - individuals do not get genuine love and happiness by murder and theft; they don't get love and happiness from a dead body. When the machine forms intellectual love and happiness the machine is not dead. Then the machine is undead - hearing the recorded speech of individuals; this means the speakers are undead by recorded sound.

The intellect is moving - motion and pressure constitutes the most basic form of life there is, for motion and pressure make life and the intellect exists; when intellect is changed there is intellectual motion - every moving body will cause different pressures within. If the intellect doesn't exist, the intellect is not known. If the intellect is detected and known, there is surely life - intelligent life. The intellect makes individuals undead by the motion and pressure that the intellect makes; there is physical motion and pressure forming intellectual life. There is intellectual motion and pressure forming moral life. Physical motion plus pressure forms intellectual feeling. Intellectual motion plus pressure forms moral existence.

The head exists without the body. Intellect stems from the body. Morality stems from the voice. The sound of the individual's voice is his personal identity. His moral body is inside the sound of his voice - every living sound has moral connection; men and women heard by recorded sound are not capable of living the same lifespan again because their existence is going forward in time. Different speech patterns are spoken so they don't live the same speech pattern again. When intellect is spoken the intellect is undead. When they depart, their recorded speech is spoken by the machine. Then they become undead.

An artificial heart pumps in a different way than a heart of flesh. The goal of the artificial heart is the same as that of the heart of flesh: the goal is what makes them alive, not the function. The recording is part of an individual. His past recordings are closer to him than yesterday. His recorded past comes first, or takes priority. His recorded past is registered by no departure. The recording is closer to him than his distant past. He does not go back to the distant past because his distant past is already recorded. If men and women prove life after death, they see what conditions are like before they get there. They are aware they are going to live the same life again - when they detect living the same lifespan again. They escape by recorded sound.

The public can have their speech recorded at the police station. The government and police will know who has committed murder, who committed theft, who committed a crime. The police will know this, because when individuals tell lies their speech is not theirs; when they tell lies the devil knows. Their talking will betray them. When they tell the truth, however, the speech is theirs; then they live by recorded sound forever - or at least until they are resurrected. When they tell lies they die, then live the same lifespan over and over again, forever.

The police will ask each individual member of the public questions - for instance, 'Did you kill, did you commit theft? Did you or are you breaking the law?' If they tell lies devils are surely doing the talking, though this does not mean that they will escape punishment by telling the truth. Punishment is better than living the same lifespan again forever. The police should be able to put up posters and signs everywhere, reminding crime makers of what can happen if they don't tell the truth.

The speech of the public can be recorded every six months at the local police station. The public can record a new speech every six months. If they intend to commit suicide the police will ask them; by telling lies they shall live the same death over and over again. It is rare for a man or woman to commit suicide on the spur of the moment, for they usually think about committing suicide first - generally six months before they commit suicide. Statistics suggest that one in 10,000 killers will commit murder. Theft, too, shall be prevented. When the public live by recorded speech they don't feel any hurt, grief, or suffering. When they live by recorded sound they feel calm, cool, even love. There is no gloom, no pain, no death, no war. The feeling of love lasts forever.

CHAPTER TEN

THE SOLUTION FOR THE ENERGY CRISIS:
THE GRAVITY ENGINE

A FALLING WEIGHT drives a permanent magnet generator. The generator produces one kilowatt of electricity. The same falling weight drops to the same distance, driving ten permanent magnet generators instead of one. This means the weight falls ten times slower because the weight is driving ten generators instead of one. The electric current produced from the generators is the same electric current as one single generator driven ten times faster. The 'magic' is that the weight falls the same distance. The one-kilowatt electric current continues ten times longer. If the falling weight drops the same distance driving 59 generators, the one-kilowatt electric current continues for a period of time 50 times longer. The weight falls the same distance. The energy produced by the falling weight lasts 50 times longer. This increases the energy time of the falling weight fifty-fold. When the energy time is increased forty-fold, the electricity from the falling weight lifts a second weight - the same height as the first. Then the second weight comes down, driving the generators; then the first weight is lifted; then the first weight comes down, driving the generators; then the second weight is lifted.

CHAPTER ELEVEN

THE RAISING OF THE DEAD

IF INDIVIDUALS ARE IN PAIN, the pain ends. If they are dead, the pain doesn't necessarily end. If they are alive the pain ends by compensation. When they are destined to become morally dead, they are already dead before they arrive. You might say they had the motion of an undead man. They had the motion of a dead man. When they become dead they always were dead; when they live the same lifespan again and again, having no awareness of where they are going, doing the same thing over and over again forever, not aware they are doing the same thing again and again, they are dead.

The dead stone doesn't make any original or independent movement. The dead stone has no awareness. The dead stone is still, moved only by other bodies not connected to the stone. Still bodies don't move by their own accord. Still bodies move by force. To live the same lifespan again, not knowing they are repeating themselves is to be dead.

At the age of 55 to 58 the awareness of the fight for life ends, after which the individuals concerned become altered, dead and stillborn. At one stage or another, a stillborn baby was alive; the baby was not alive in this world; then, according to the doctor, the baby always was dead. Men and women were alive in the animal world. They are not alive in the world of the immortal. By realising they are doing the same thing again, they are forced to do the same thing repeatedly. They are not forced morally. This means they are not doing the same thing over and over again morally; if they are not doing the same thing morally, they are not doing the same thing again absolutely. When they are doing the same thing again morally, they are dead; when they are not doing the same morally, they are undead.

When they are undead they are aware of pain and suffering. If they are aware they are undead, they are indeed undead; then sooner or later the suffering, pain and grief ends, forever. The dead are raised by proof of repeated lifespans - and the drinking of water alone. Sweet drinks distract the awareness. As soon as they discover living repeated lifespans, they forget.

The following pages may not interest you. The technologies in this book are for the eyes of the scientists. Again I tell you to issue this book to the appropriate persons - namely, doctors, scientists, the police, the media, local politicians, solicitors, companies. The government has got to be alerted.

CHAPTER TWELVE

A SIMPLE PERPETUAL MOTION ENGINE

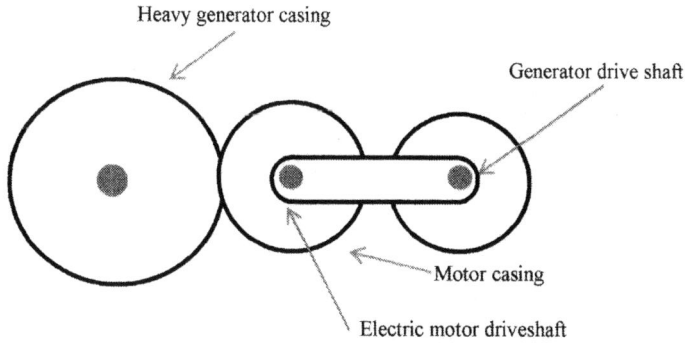

Heavy generator casing

Generator drive shaft

Motor casing

Electric motor driveshaft

THE GENERATOR is 20 times heavier than the electric motor. Both the action and reaction of the electric motor are put to use. The casing of the electric motor drives a heavy generator - 20 times heavier than itself. As a result the drive shaft of the electric motor rotates at almost maximum speed; the drive shaft of the electric motor drives a second generator 20 times lighter than the heavier generator.

When the electric motor and generators are in outer space and earth orbit and beyond the gravitational effect of the very heavy generator and light generator, they produce more electricity than the battery. Then the battery is replaced by electricity coming from both generators. The perpetual motion engine can be used to supply electricity to satellites, and spacecraft. The perpetual motion engine can supply power to space stations. The perpetual motion works in outer space alone. The engine in outer space is more efficient than the gravity engine.

CHAPTER THIRTEEN

A ROBOT FOR RESURRECTION

PART OF THE CREDIT of the robot is the fact the robot recognises any spoken word and recognises any object within sight. This is how the ears work. An individual speaks the word; then a machine records the word and voice pattern. In the region of 1000 to 10,000 different words are recorded. Because the voice pattern of each word is recorded by one individual, when the individual speaks the word, the voice pattern of the word always matches the voice pattern of the word by the same person. The machine is then told the meaning of the word by a second computer.

This is how the eyes work. A television is placed onto a touch sensitive light panel - the same as they use in supermarkets. When customers touch the screen with their fingers, the panel flicks to a different function. When customers touch the screen, no light shines on that particular part of the machine's screen. This is why the machine is activated, flicking to the next function. The television screen is processing against the light panel. When there are dark parts on the television screen, those patches are in fact showing less light - so they appear as darker patches on those particular parts of the light panel. This causes the light panel to activate a numbered image for those particular parts of the television screen. The image on the television vision screen changes constantly - within a fraction of a second. The wizard is withholding details of how to make the robot that will recognise different sights outside the darkroom. The wizard will release full details of the eyes of the robot after the government has paid the wizard's demands.

This is how the body of the robot works. A man wears a mechanical suit. The man performs different body movements. The suit then measures the different body movements. The man records anything from 1000 to 50,000 different body movements. Each individual body movement is measured and then recorded. The recorded body movements are then placed inside the robot's memory. Then electric motors inside the robot's body move the robot to take up the exact positions the robot is programmed for, in accordance with those made by the person wearing the suit. The suit is made to record the different tasks and actions performed by the wearer; for instance, the man lifts a bucket and opens a door; then the robot knows how to carry out particular tasks and actions. The robot android is educated (programmed) to apply the approximate body movements and actions for the task. Physical actions are recorded. The next time the robot is told to do the same recorded action the robot 'knows' what to do. Details of how to make the robot obey any physical command and do any job, as well as obeying intellectual commands and doing intellectual jobs, will be made available by the wizard.

The wizard will make available full details after the demands of the wizard are paid; a full understanding of how the robot android works will be issued to the government when the wizard's demands are paid. In short, no robot, no resurrection.

Resurrection is supernatural. Scientists have unusual powers, not supernatural powers. Only the wizard of this book can issue the instructions for resurrection. There is one single wizard born once in a number of past generations, and the same applies to future generations. The wizard is a freak - a zebra born without stripes. This happens rarely - perhaps even once and never again.

The robot can do any job - drive cars, collect children from school, do the washing, cooking, cleaning, do the shopping, pay the bills. If the government pays my demands, immediately, I'll issue the robot.

CHAPTER FOURTEEN

DISORDERS AND DEMANDS

BY PAYING the simple easy-to-pay demands of the wizard, the world never has to work again. The population can put their feet to rest. A non-working population is a whole world higher than a working population. If the government doesn't pay the demands of the wizard, the public will be angry - knowing a robot could have been doing their job.

Within the next 12 to 14 years millions of robots can be rolling off the production line - perhaps within the next nine to ten years. The wizard has a health condition. If his body of flesh should die there will be no resurrection for anybody. Only the wizard can issue the technology for resurrection - and then even he may realise resurrection is impossible for him to achieve. There is no proof of living forever after resurrection - and there is proof of staying undead by recorded sound. The wizard is standing by his claim to provide the know-how for the promotion of the undead by recorded speech. The wizard is certain, or confident of living the same lifespan again and again.

Religious men and women have no fear of living repeated lifespans when they accept the man who died on the cross 2000 years ago - and when they worship their maker. Many in the United Kingdom worship their maker through the Church of England protestant religion: they have joy and no fear of living futile repeated lifespans. Opposing the maker of man and opposing the man that died on the cross 2000 years ago will result in the fear of living repeated lifespans. The pain and fear will increase.

The government is not above religion; doctors, scientists, the media, film makers, are not above religion. The truth comes from the maker of man; no maker dies and lives the same lifespan over and over again. Those who have the famous spacecraft motion will know that motion has no beginning and has no end. The motion was here countless eons ago. The motion comes from the maker of man, not from men. When they reject their maker, the motion they had ends. If they comply with the motion by reluctance of force, they are not part of the motion; if they don't believe the maker of man, they respond to the motion by force. This brings me to a disorder the governments are not aware of - and which the public are not aware of. The maker of man said, 'Come to me with all your spiritual problems.' Psychiatrists say, 'Come to us - we shall give you drugs, we know better.' The man who died on the cross 2000 years ago told the public, 'Rest your weary head with me.' Psychiatrists say, 'Rest your head with us, we shall give you drugs - we know better.' They have full awareness that they contravene the man who died on the cross 2000 years ago, saying they know better.

Psychiatrists boast they are doctors of the mind, but they are men and men don't have a mind; they have no understanding of the mind. The man who died on the cross 2000 years ago had a true understanding of the soul, not the mind. Psychiatrists ask men and women, 'How are you in your spirits?' Man has one single spirit - not many - and has no understanding of the spirit. Psychiatrists never mention the soul for this will bring them into conflict with religion. Psychiatrists have no understanding of the soul. Psychiatrists speak of the person, saying he or she is suffering from a personality disorder. The person is physical. What is physical is not disorderly - there is never such a thing as person disorders. Psychiatrists say a man is suffering from a mental disorder, but a famous religious book tells us that man has a spirit, not a mind. The man who died on the cross 2000 years ago did not recommend drugs for the mind and spirit. The maker of man issued a famous religious book in which he did not tell men and women to treat the mind and spirit by drugs.

Either the individuals that make up the government worship their maker or they worship the devil or Satan. There is no choice of a position between the maker of man and Satan or the devil. Sitting on the fence between the two is not an option. If men and women don't read, their speech is not theirs when they have their speech recorded. Call a man superman - he shall receive fresh nervous energy, but he is not superman; call a psychiatrist doctor - he shall receive fresh nervous energy, but he knows he is not a doctor: psychiatrists resort to forcing drugs on their patients so they can call themselves doctors. Doctors issue drugs, and this is why they issue drugs: they know the drugs make matters extremely worse.

Religious men and women have a wider understanding of a divided soul. Psychiatrists have a divided soul. Psychiatrists don't know what the person is. Psychiatrists don't know what the soul is. Psychiatrists don't know what the spirit is. Psychiatrists don't know what the mind is. The dog barks by feeling - the dog has no understanding of what men and women arc talking about. Psychiatrists have no understanding of what they are doing and talking about. The government is wasting taxpayers' money - by paying psychiatrists thousands of pounds a week for making matters considerably worse; psychiatrists' mental asylum staff and social workers have been fooling the public and government for decades, stealing or sapping nervous energy from those under their care. The police ought to be the ones who control and run mental asylums - they have a better understanding of intentional and unintentional disorders. Psychiatrists have a salary of 2000 pounds a week while social workers are calling upon the police to have innocent men and women placed in mental asylums. Previously they had no powers. Today they are part of the mental health fraternity.

Psychiatrists and social workers are injecting chemicals into the wizard's body. The injections they force onto the patient cut short the victim's life by 15 to 30 years. Yet they purport to know the man that died on the cross 2000 years ago. Is the cure for the head? They know they don't know better and therefore know they are committing murder by reducing the victim's life by 15 to 30 years.

This in effect makes them killers, not life bringers. The truth comes from the maker of man; if they don't believe their maker, they don't speak the truth. They have committed life-threatening perjury against the wizard. All of them are liars having no truth, whereas the wizard has five religious certificates and speaks the truth. If the wizard succumbs to the pressure of their drugs and dies, there will be no artificial body, no robot for the future, and no guarantee of life perpetuated through resurrection; the public will remain undead by recorded sound, then be trapped in living the same life again. Governments are putting the lives of the public at risk, not to mention the wizard's life.

The longer the government ignores the warning of this book, the closer the wizard approaches the state of being undead. The government should act immediately. If the government wants to save lives and relieve the public from sterile nine-to-five jobs, it needs to give the message of this book due consideration.

CHAPTER FIFTEEN

DISORDERS AND ADVICE

THE GOVERNMENT is fully aware that smoking ruins lives. The government knows smokers require their cigarettes to make them feel relaxed, confident, at ease; the government knows when they have no cigarettes they feel they are not going to survive - they think being deprived of nicotine is the end of the world: they feel pain, frustration, even become violent and angry. Yet the government is refusing to help them.

There are two explanations why the government doesn't make smoking illegal. The first is that the government might otherwise lose voters; the second is that the government is afraid of smokers: they fear the public they govern. The government ought to have made smoking illegal 50 years ago. Non-smokers are forced to put up with passive smoking - when they walk the streets, when they are at home and at work. Doctors had the power to force the government to make smoking illegal but they did not take the initiative and now the spark of that initiative has gone out.

Smoking is a disorderly sight to see, the opposite of life. Non-smokers are forced to have a whiff of smoke going down their lungs as they walk the streets. Smokers don't give a damn who they choke, as long as they are smoking. Smoking is what one might describe as disorderly behaviour; when people smoke walking along the street, displaying their disgusting habit, they are committing a repulsive action because they are forcing others to breathe in their smoke. This is not short of bullying. Non-smokers are the ones who have to pay the extra hospital costs, and the government has been ignoring this smoking disorder.

If smoking continues the government is not doing their job effectively. If smokers go back in time and are seen there, smoking, by the maker, they shall be slaughtered! If smokers go forward in time they shall be judged by the maker. When they do the opposite of what they are designed to do, they abuse their religious or the divine purpose, doing the opposite of what they're designed for. Smokers consider themselves gay by smoking, but the maker of man is not going to allow them to smoke and live forever at the same time. When they refuse to end their stupid actions - their behaviour and conduct - their mistaken lifestyle won't allow them to live forever. If the government refuses to end smoking, they are also harming the health of non-smokers.

CHAPTER SIXTEEN

THE MARK OF LIFE

GOING BACK to the spacecraft motion discussed at the beginning of Chapter Five ('The Unextinct Human Race'), the spacecraft motion forms perpetual motion amongst stars and planets like a chain reaction; the resultant motion of space also forms a small mark - when space dust, debris, comets, planets and stars are affected and collide, partly caused by the spacecraft's motion. The impact of the colliding planets, space dust, debris, stars, comets, moons, asteroids forms a mark, partly coming from the perpetual spacecraft motion. The mark never happens in one place alone - the motion of the stars and planets and moons and space dust, debris and comets and asteroids spreads across the galaxy and universe forever, for an unlimited number of miles and light years.

Part of the motion comes from the spacecraft - the collision of objects and mass in space, which spreads across the galaxies forming a mark by each individual collision. There is always a fresh new individual mark made at different places across the universe. Space scientists, rocket scientists, space technicians, space engineers - and space advocates and space society members - are partly responsible for the mark: the spacecraft was launched and seen by these who are part of the space movement. This means that space persons have the mark of life - they're not aware of what they have done until they either discover or are told what they have done. When they realise they have the mark of life they don't end - they're not altered - because in a sense part of them is perpetuated and seen in the sky forever. The mark is part of them. Part of them is seen forever. Consequently part of them never ends. Then they realise they have contributed to eternity, or what one might call the sight of forever.

At the age of 48 there is an absolute end of the sight of forever, when every man will foresee the end of everything at the age of 48. There's no detection of forever at the age of 48. After they realise they have the mark, they are able to detect forever and do so at all ages: 50, 60, 80, 90, 120 - all ages. When they see forever they have forever. Then they don't become altered - because part of them is not altered: the mark is a whole world above the spacecraft motion; when they know they have the motion they are not extinguished; when they detect they have the mark they are not altered. This means they continue to remember into eternity.

At the age of 48 they don't remember where they came from - the memory of youth is no more. They don't remember youth, but they remember they are alive. When they don't remember the best they can achieve is to be considered undead. At the age of 55 they become dead, extinguished, as it were, because they have proof of their mortality; yet at the age of 65 they become obliterated because the old man has put on immortality by virtue of the mark of life.

CHAPTER SEVENTEEN

THE WATER OF LIFE

MEN AND WOMEN are drinking sweet drinks. Sweet drinks are the opposite of life. Animals drink water for sanity. They know if they drink sweet water they become crazy, crazy, insane. They have an instinctive aversion for sweet drinks, knowing sweet drinks are death; animals know if they drink sweet drinks they lose and destroy their instincts - then they don't escape the lion inside their body; animals fear drinking sweet drinks for they know if they drink sweet drinks they don't make any sense. Ask an animal to drink sweet drinks and you will have a fight on your hands; the animal may even respond with the intent to kill. This all goes to show that men and women are not doing what is sane by drinking sweetened drinks. As a result the public are not sane.

A sane man will strive to prove there is life after death - an afterlife. He will not stop trying to prove this until he has proof - if this takes 30 years, so be it. Members of the public are doing everything in half measures. They are not going the full way. Sane men and women have the natural inclination to live as long as they can. Members of the public are going part of the way - refusing to make the effort for age extension. The sane have the natural inclination to live as long as they can, whereas the insane will not make the effort to strive for any form of age extension. It's logical to want to live as long as you can - insanity to ignore the quest for age extension by failing to go the full way. To seek longevity or the preservation of life in an afterlife by going only part of the way and then refusing to make the effort for further age extension is insane. Sane men and women live as long as they can.

When men and women drink sweet drinks, they don't want to live; they don't want to die, of course, since they are either ignorant or prepared to ignore the implication of imbibing death. Perhaps they are simply unaware of how sickening sweet drinks are until they drink water. Sweet drinks kill the desire to extend their age - and kill the desire to live.

People have the desire to live when their lives are threatened, as when they are involved in an accident; yet when the accident has ended and they are out of danger, they go back to having no desire to live. A famous religious book has prophesied that people will put all detestable things in a cup and drink it; if sweet drinks are disgusting then nauseating things like aspartamine and saccharine are in the cup. The famous religious book has told the readers the water of life provided by the man that died on the cross 2000 years ago was turned into wine at a wedding feast. Today the water of life has been made impure, and instead of being fit for wine from the true vine, has been polluted and poisoned. Water was at the beginning of life, and poison is at the end.

Doctors are drinking tea and coffee, then claiming they know what's healthy. The human body wasn't designed for hot drinks, but doctors don't see any physical harm in them and consider what they are drinking is healthy. Do they know they are making assumptions that might lead to intellectual and moral harm? By the same token lesbians and homosexuals don't see any physical harm in the unnatural acts in which they engage, acts that are not in accordance with the body's design for reproduction, then say what they are doing is healthy while they know they are morally crazy.

CHAPTER EIGHTEEN

CORRECTIONS

NEWTON'S LAW OF MOTION *maintains that for every action there is an equal and opposite reaction.* Mr Newton was not correct. For every natural action there is an equal and opposite reaction, but for every artificial action there is no equal and opposite reaction. The levitating space vehicle discussed in this book moves by action-action. Action-action motion doesn't end. The perpetual spacecraft motion mentioned in this book doesn't end, as has already been clarified. Action-action motion already exists, or pre-exists. A rocket is launched by human motion, and the rocket launches the spacecraft; this means human motion is action-action motion. The motion of animals results in an equal and opposite reaction, whereas the actions of humans have a ripple effect that continues forever, like a chain reaction. Humans have been speaking the word of creation, the *logos*, forever, since the beginning; animals don't perform actions that continue forever because they have no understanding of forever, or eternity.

Time doesn't slow down by speed or velocity. Forward time is relative to forward time - no difference is made by increasing the velocity of the vehicle; when a vehicle attains the velocity of light there is no slowing down of time aboard the star vehicle. Albert Einstein was saying because the motion of the vehicle is so fast, the motion is not relative; a good deed is relative to a good deed - this makes no difference how good the deed is. A star vehicle travelling at the velocity of light is relative to a car travelling at 10 mph - if the motion of the star vehicle is not relative, the motion of the star vehicle is not motion; if the picture is not relative to pictures, the picture is not a picture.

A star vehicle shall travel faster than light. When a star vehicle approaches the speed or velocity of light, the size of the star vehicle doesn't increase; this is because if the size of the star vehicle increases, the explosion or what propels the star vehicle increases with the star vehicle relative to the size of the explosion; as the explosion increases, it yields more energy, and when the explosion yields more energy the vehicle continues to accelerate at the same rate as light photons accelerate at the speed of light. If Albert's theory is correct, light photons will grow to the size of the galaxy and larger than the galaxy. There are no speed and velocity limits.

Scientists are not going to make any constructive sense by drinking toxic, poisoned arsenic drinks - namely tea and coffee, however diluted and fizzy; from poisonous drinks come nonsense. Albert was not a genius because genius is sane, reaching or striving for health, a love of life - not smoking and drinking poisonous drinks. All of Albert Einstein's theories are nonsensical, and since they amount to nonsense they are not sane; when they make nonsense there is no alternative. The alternative of sweet drinks is the drinking of water alone.

There was no Big Bang. The ingredients of the Big Bang were there before the Big Bang. The ingredients had motion. Motion has no beginning and has no end. Mass doesn't come from nothing - the mass has always been there. The mass has, and always has had motion. This means the universe has always been here.

The universe is not expanding. The universe is too large to expand. This book has proven the universe is an unlimited number of years old. This means if the universe is expanding, the universe has been expanding forever. This means the universe has unlimited size - meaning the universe is not capable of expanding because the universe is already filling the space before the universe reaches its parameters. What has unlimited size never expands; when water is drunk the drinkers have awareness of forever at all ages; when they drink sweet drinks they are aware of forever - until they reach the age of 48; at the age of 48 there is an absolute end of everything.

There are no black holes. There are no black holes for mass doesn't vanish. What exists, exists forever. Scientists telling us there are black holes when they don't have proof is bending the truth; telling us there are black holes that suck everything in so that not even light can escape expresses a fear of physics, or imparts a fear of physics; fear of physics is not acceptable - there is proof mass does not simply vanish. If mass goes out of existence, it never existed in the first place. When scientists refuse the drinking of water they don't make any constructive sense - they make sense by physical intellect, not intellectual intellect; they see smoking as bad for the physical body, having no awareness - one puff, then all awareness of life is lost.

CHAPTER NINETEEN

THE SOUND OF LOVE

GOING BACK to perpetual motion and the spacecraft that left the solar system travelling towards another star discussed at the beginning of Chapter Five: it was said that the spacecraft motion causes planets, stars, space dust and debris to collide. The collision forms a small mark and when a mark is made there is a sound; marks are made by physical contact - and physical contact makes sound. The sound travels all over the galaxies forever and ever. Sound that continues forever exists; sound that doesn't continue forever doesn't exist. The sound of animals doesn't exist; this is why animals don't know what they are talking about. Men and women are not above religion until they are aware of the sound of love; a famous religious book went as far as the mark of life, as was discussed in Chapter Nineteen ('The Mark of Life'). The sound of love is higher than the mark of life. The mark is the record, and the record is the soul; the sound of love is the Spirit, and the Spirit is Love. Love is the maker of man. The soul is either satisfaction or life. The soul is the World, but motion is Limbo. Limbo is the body. The motion is life, and life is the body.

Printed in Great Britain
by Amazon